Dirty Bertie

FANGS!

For Simon – thanks for my "SURPRISE"
birthday song ~ D R
For all Bertie fans – and especially those who
have written me letters ~ A M

STRIPES PUBLISHING
An imprint of Little Tiger Press
1 The Coda Centre, 189 Munster Road,
London SW6 6AW

A paperback original
First published in Great Britain in 2010

Characters created by David Roberts
Text copyright © Alan MacDonald, 2010
Illustrations copyright © David Roberts, 2010

ISBN: 978-1-84715-139-1

Printed and bound in the UK

10 9 8

Dirty Bertie
FANGS!

DAVID ROBERTS WRITTEN BY ALAN MACDONALD

Stripes

Collect all the
Dirty Bertie books!

Contents

CHAPTER 1

It was Book Week at Bertie's school and everyone had come dressed as their favourite character. Bertie looked round the playground. There were four witches, a sprinkling of fairies and a rash of Harry Potters. Darren was dressed as Dennis the Menace. Eugene was Willy Wonka. Bertie smiled to himself. His costume

was better than any of them. He was
Count Dracula. He had a black cloak and
a pair of plastic fangs. A rubber bat
dangled from his wrist like a yo-yo.

"Who are you?" asked Eugene.

Bertie glared. "Who do you think?"

"Dunno. The Big Bad Wolf?"

"I'm Count Dracula!" said Bertie.

"Dracula doesn't wear trainers," said
Darren.

Suddenly, a dark shadow
fell over them.

"Good morning!" said a sinister voice.

Bertie turned round. He gasped. Yikes, it was another vampire! And this one was taller and ten times as scary!

"Heh heh! Did I frighten you?" laughed the vampire, taking out his fangs.

"Mr Grouch!" said Bertie.

"Count Grouch," corrected the caretaker. "I see you had the same idea. Spooky, eh?"

He looked down at something by Bertie's foot.

"What's that?"

"Um … a sweet wrapper," said Bertie.

"LITTER! Pick it up!"

"But I didn't…"

"PICK IT UP!" snapped Mr Grouch.

"And don't ever drop litter in my playground. I have my eye on you."

He put in his fangs and swept away, trailing his cape behind him.

"Yikes!" shivered Eugene. "He scared me to death!"

"Me too," said Darren. "How does he sneak up like that?"

Bertie scowled. "It's not fair! Dracula was my idea!"

"Yeah, but his costume's better," said Darren. "I thought he *was* a vampire."

"Maybe he is," said Eugene.

Darren and Bertie stared at him.

"What do you mean?"

"Well," said Eugene, "yesterday I passed his shed – the one he always keeps locked. Mr Grouch was sitting outside, having a drink."

Darren shrugged. "So? What's funny about that?"

"It's what he was drinking," said Eugene. "It looked like … *blood*!"

"BLOOD?" gasped Bertie.

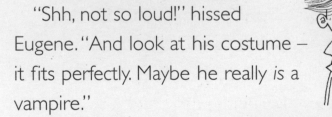

"Shh, not so loud!" hissed Eugene. "And look at his costume – it fits perfectly. Maybe he really *is* a vampire."

"But vampires can't stand the daylight," Darren objected.

"Maybe he's a kind of half vampire," suggested Bertie. "Half vampire, half caretaker."

It made sense. Bertie had always thought there was something creepy about the school caretaker. He had staring eyes for a start – and no hair. He hated children (Bertie especially). Plus he had a weird habit of suddenly appearing, like a ghost.

"We've got to stop him!" said Bertie.

"He hasn't done anything yet," said Darren, "except clean the toilets."

"How do you know?" said Bertie. "How do you know he's not murderin' teachers and drinking their blood? What about Miss Withers?"

Miss Withers had taught Class 2 – until she had gone home sick and never returned. Or that was what people said. But what if Mr Grouch had murdered her and hidden the body? It was a worrying thought.

Eugene fingered his neck uneasily. "What shall we do?" he asked.

"Spy on him," said Bertie. "Find out what he's up to. We'll take it in turns."

"Good idea," said Darren. "You go first."

"ME? Why me?" said Bertie.

"It's your idea. And anyway, he hates you already."

CHAPTER 2

All that morning, Bertie kept an eye on
Mr Grouch through the window. He
wrote down everything he saw in the
back of his maths book.

Vampire Report
9.15 a.m. Grouch sweeping up litter
10.00 a.m. No vampire sitings
10.35 a.m. Has cup of tea and choclate biscit (DARK choclate)
11.15 a.m. Hasn't bitten ennyone - yet
11.30 a.m. Goes into shed
11.32 a.m. Comes out with mop and buckit

Dirty Bertie

After lunch, Bertie hung around the
shed, hoping to spy on the caretaker.
It wasn't long before Mr Grouch
appeared, wearing his usual scowl.
He was still dressed in his
black vampire's cape.

Bertie ducked behind the shed out of
sight. He heard Mr Grouch unlock the
door and go inside. A minute later, the
caretaker returned with a bag and a
folding chair. He sat down in the sunshine
and began to eat his sandwiches.

Bertie crept to the
corner of the shed and
peeped out. Mr Grouch
was reaching into his bag.
He brought out an old
green Thermos and
poured something into
a plastic cup. Bertie
gasped. It was bright
red and steaming slightly... BLOOD!

Eugene was right. There was no
escaping the horrible truth – Mr Grouch
was a vampire.

Bertie found Darren and Eugene waiting
for him in the playground.

"Blood?" said Darren, when he'd given
his report. "You're sure?"

"Course I'm sure, I saw him drink it!" said Bertie.

"So whose blood was it?"

"How do I know?"

"I told you he's a vampire!" said Eugene. "We should go to Miss Skinner!"

"Oh yeah, she's *really* going to believe us," said Darren.

Bertie shook his head. "First we need evidence. We've got to actually prove he's a vampire."

"How?" asked Eugene. "He's not drinking any of *my* blood!"

"Nor mine," said Darren.

Bertie frowned, thinking hard. Where would Mr Grouch hide anything he wanted to keep secret?

"The SHED!" cried Bertie. "I bet there's all kinds of stuff in there!"

"Like dead bodies!" said Darren.

"Or skeletons!" said Bertie.

Eugene turned pale. "But we're not allowed in there, and anyway he keeps it locked."

Bertie had forgotten that. Mr Grouch kept the keys in his pocket and never let them out of his sight.

"We'll have to wait till he's busy," he said. "Then we'll 'borrow' his keys and break into the shed."

CHAPTER 3

Mr Grouch was working in the Boys Toilets. A notice on the door said "CLOSED FOR REPAIRS". Bertie, Darren and Eugene stood outside, whispering.

"You keep him talking, while I look for the keys," said Bertie.

Eugene trembled. "What if he catches us?"

"Yeah. What if he tries to bite us?" said Darren.

"He won't," said Bertie. "Not while there are teachers about."

It was now or never. Bertie pushed open the door and the three of them crept in. Mr Grouch was up a ladder fixing a light.

"Oh, sorry!" said Bertie. "We, um … just needed the toilet!"

"Can't you READ?" snapped Mr Grouch. "You'll have to wait."

"Okay!" gulped Eugene.

"Actually, I'm bursting," said Bertie, "and Darren needs a poo…"

"I SAID, COME BACK LATER!" roared Mr Grouch.

They backed away towards the door. Bertie stopped. Mr Grouch's toolbox lay on the floor and on top was a set of silver keys. Bertie stumbled and pretended to trip over.

CRASH!

"Watch where you're going!" groaned
Mr Grouch.

"Sorry!" Bertie bent over and put
away the tools that he'd spilled.

A minute later, he joined the
other two outside.

"A fat lot of good
that was," said Darren.

"Oh, I don't know."
Bertie smiled. He held up his
hand, dangling a large bunch of keys.

Mr Grouch's shed stood by itself in a
corner of the playground. It was strictly
out of bounds. Bertie fiddled with the
keys, trying to find the right one.

"Hurry up!" moaned Eugene. "What
if someone comes?"

"I'm being as quick as I can!"

At last Bertie tried a small silver key. It turned with a click and the padlock sprang open. He pulled back the door and they stepped inside.

"What a dump!" said Bertie. The shed was piled high with boxes, buckets and tins. A jumble of old paint pots littered the floor. On the walls hung Mr Grouch's collection of brooms, rakes and mops.

Darren looked around. "There's nothing here!"

"Okay, we've seen it, let's go!" begged Eugene.

"Wait, there must be something," said Bertie. "We've got to find evidence."

Eugene kept a lookout by the door, while the other two searched.

Dirty Bertie

Bertie found Mr Grouch's dirty overalls hanging on a hook. Next to them was his bag. Inside was a newspaper, some gardening gloves, a lunch box – and Mr Grouch's old green Thermos.

"Look at this!" cried Bertie, excitedly.

"Open it," said Darren.

Bertie unscrewed the lid. The Thermos was empty, but the inside was smeared with bright red stains. He sniffed it. It smelled oddly familiar.

"Well?" asked Darren.

"Blood," nodded Bertie. "There's our proof!"

Eugene yelped. A tall figure in a cloak was marching across the playground towards them.

"IT'S GROUCH!" cried Eugene. "RUN!"

Dirty Bertie

Darren and Eugene bolted out of the door. Bertie looked round in panic. He stuffed the things back into Mr Grouch's bag, keeping the Thermos as evidence. But just as he reached the door, a dark figure blocked his path. Mr Grouch's eyes blazed like fire.

"What do you think you're doing?" he growled. "Did you take my keys?"

"N-n-no," stammered Bertie.

"Liar! Hand 'em over!"

"It's no good," said Bertie. "We know! We've got proof!"

"Proof?"

"That you're a vampire!" said Bertie.

"Don't be an idiot!" cried Mr Grouch. "Give me those keys – I won't ask you again."

He took a step closer. Bertie could see

his mad, staring eyes and deadly fangs.

This is it, he thought. *I'm going to be murdered, fanged to death! I have to escape!*

"YEEEARGHHHHH!" He rushed at the vampire, knocking him off balance. Mr Grouch stepped back into a paint pot and fell over.

Dirty Bertie

Bertie burst out of the shed door and slammed it shut.

CLICK! He snapped the padlock closed and ran for his life.

"HEY!" yelled Mr Grouch. "LET ME OUT!"

CHAPTER 4

Back in the classroom, Bertie stared out
of the window. Miss Boot — or Winnie
the Witch as she was today — was
droning on about homework. Across the
playground, noises came from the shed.

THUMP! THUMP! BANG!

Mr Grouch had been locked in the
shed for an hour and he sounded cross.

Luckily, Miss Boot paid no attention.
She seemed to think the caretaker was
mending a fence.

Someone poked Bertie in the back.

"What if he gets out?" hissed Eugene.

"He can't!"

"But what if he does? He saw you,
Bertie!"

THUMP! Was it Bertie's imagination
or were the noises getting louder?

THUMP! BANG! CLUNK!

Mr Grouch was trying to break the
door down. Maybe vampires had the
strength of ten men?

"BERTIE!" boomed Miss Boot. "STOP
STARING OUT OF THE WINDOW!
GET ON WITH YOUR WORK!"

Bertie tried to concentrate. He looked
at what he'd scribbled in his science book.

THE EARTH GOES ROUND THE SUN.
THE SUN IS BIG AND RED.
LIKE BLOOD...

He glanced back out of the window.
ARGH! The shed door was open and
hanging off its hinges. Grouch had
escaped! Bertie's heart beat faster.
He glanced around. *Don't panic*, he
thought. *Miss Boot's here and even
vampires are afraid of her. Anyway, he
won't come into class…*

WHAM!

The door burst open. Mr Grouch
stood there, red-faced and furious.
His cape was torn and his trousers were
splashed with paint. Eugene let out a
scream.

"Mr Grouch!" cried Miss Boot. "What on earth…?"

The caretaker stormed into the room. "Where's that boy?" he panted. "Just let me get my hands on him!"

Bertie was trying to slide down under his desk. But Mr Grouch spotted him.

"YOU!" he yelled. "I want a word with you!"

Dirty Bertie

Miss Boot barred his way. "Mr Grouch! You are interrupting my class! What is this about?"

"Ask him!" said Mr Grouch, pointing at Bertie. "He stole my keys. He locked me in the shed!"

Miss Boot glared. "BERTIE! Is that true?"

"I had to," said Bertie. "He's a vampire! He's murderin' people!"

Mr Grouch rolled his eyes. "It's a costume, you dope – for Book Week!"

"Don't listen to him!" said Bertie, desperately. "He drinks blood! We've seen him!"

"BLOOD?" said Mr Grouch. "What are you talking about?"

"This," said Bertie. He reached under his desk and brought out the Thermos. He tipped it up to show everyone the inside. "See? RED! Those are bloodstains!"

Mr Grouch snorted. "That's tomato soup!"

"W-what?" gulped Bertie.

"Soup! Tomato soup. I have it for my lunch."

Dirty Bertie

"Not … blood?" Bertie sniffed it.
He knew the smell was familiar. Oops!
If it wasn't blood, then Mr Grouch wasn't
really a vampire. He was just a hopping
mad caretaker who Bertie had locked in
a shed for over an hour. Bertie backed
away. There was only one thing for it…

"BERTIE!" yelled Miss Boot. "COME
BACK HERE!"

CHAPTER 1

Bertie hunched over his breakfast cereal, his hair flopping in his eyes.

SLURP! MUNCH! CRUNCH!

Mum looked up.

"BERTIE!" she sighed.

"What?"

"Your hair!"

"What's wrong with it?"

"It's a mess!"

Bertie tipped his head back. "It looks okay to me."

"I'm surprised you can see anything," said Mum. "You need a haircut!"

"NOOO!" cried Bertie. He HATED having his hair cut. He liked his hair just the way it was. Scruffy. Messy. Dirty. Bertie never combed his hair or brushed it. He howled whenever his mum washed it. As for haircuts – ugh, why bother? Weren't his parents always moaning about saving money? If he gave up haircuts it would save them thousands of pounds. They ought to be grateful. They ought to be giving him more pocket money, rather than complaining!

Dad looked at Mum. "Are you going to take him?"

Dirty Bertie

"Certainly not," said Mum. "It's your turn."

"It's not!"

"It is! I took him last time, remember?"

Mum wasn't likely to forget. Bertie had nits at the time, though they only found out when the hairdresser screamed. They hadn't been back there since.

"Anyway," she said. "I don't get home in time."

Dirty Bertie

Dad groaned. "All right, I'll take him after school."

Bertie looked horrified.

"I can't!" he moaned. "I … I've got homework!"

"That never stops you watching TV," snorted Dad. "We'll go to Bob's on the high street."

Bertie nearly choked on his cereal. Bob? Not *Sweeney Bob* the barber? Darren had

gone there and he'd come back looking like a hedgehog! Everyone had called him Spike for weeks!

"Not there!" said Bertie.

"It's fine," said Dad. "Lots of people go there."

"*You* don't!" said Bertie.

"No, well I get my hair cut at Super Snips," said Dad. "It's, um … easier."

Super Snips was the smart new hairdresser's in town. Eugene went there with his mum. They had comfy chairs and comics, and they handed out free lollipops to children. The only thing Sweeney Bob handed out was a tissue to wipe your neck.

"Why can't I go to Super Snips?" asked Bertie.

"Too posh," said Mum.

"Too expensive," said Dad.

"Anyway, I don't see why you're making such a fuss, Bertie," said Mum. "And Dad could do with a haircut, too.

Why don't you both go together?"

"No, thanks," said Dad quickly. "Mine can wait."

"So can mine," said Bertie. "I think it's stopped growing!"

Mum gave him a look. "Bertie, you are getting a haircut and that's final."

Bertie sighed heavily and stomped upstairs.

He looked at his reflection in the bathroom mirror. What was wrong with his hair, anyway? He liked it getting in his eyes. It was a pity he wasn't born before haircuts were invented. Cavemen went around looking as hairy as apes. Bertie thought he would have made a good caveman.

He stared at himself, trying to imagine his face without any hair. Darren would

Dirty Bertie

laugh his socks off. "Ugly," they'd call him
at school. "Baldybum." He'd have to go
around with a bag over his head.

CHAPTER 2

After school, Eugene came back to Bertie's house.

Dad was in the kitchen, working on his computer.

"Dad!" said Bertie. "Can Eugene come to play?"

"Not today, I'm taking you for a haircut, remember?"

Dirty Bertie

Bertie groaned. He was hoping bringing Eugene back would give him an excuse to stay at home.

"But Eugene's here," he said.

"So I see."

"Hello, Mr Burns!" said Eugene.

"Can't he stay – just for a bit?" begged Bertie.

"My mum says it's okay," said Eugene.

Dad looked at his watch. "All right!" he sighed. "But just for half an hour. The barber shuts at five."

Eugene and Bertie ran upstairs before Dad changed his mind. Bertie slammed the door.

"What's wrong?" said Eugene.

"Didn't you hear?" groaned Bertie. "I've got to have my hair cut."

"So? What's so bad about that?"

"At the barber's," said Bertie.
"Sweeney Bob's."

Eugene looked at him.

"HA HA!" he hooted. "I can't wait to
see you tomorrow!"

"It's not funny," moaned Bertie.

"Why don't you go to Super Snips?"
said Eugene.

"I've tried that," said Bertie. "Dad
won't take me. You've got to help me."

Bertie racked his brains. There had to
be some way out. His eyes fell on the
kitchen scissors he'd borrowed to cut
out some dinosaur pictures. Of course!
Mum and Dad wanted him to have a
haircut, so why not have one? He could
cut it himself! Wait, though, maybe that
wasn't such a great idea. It would be
impossible to see what he was doing.

Dirty Bertie

Much safer to get someone else to do it
– and luckily he knew just the person.

"Eugene," said Bertie. "I've got a great
idea…"

Dirty Bertie

Five minutes later, Bertie sat in a chair with a towel draped around his shoulders. Eugene hesitated.

"Are you sure about this?" he asked, doubtfully.

"Of course, I told you!" said Bertie.

"But what if I get in trouble? If your dad finds out, he'll kill us!"

"He won't," said Bertie. "Anyway, he *wants* me to have my hair cut!"

"Yes, but not by me," said Eugene. "I've never done this before!"

"It's easy!" said Bertie. "It's like cutting paper. Hurry up, before anyone comes!"

Eugene took a deep breath. He had a bad feeling about this. He chose a long hair sticking up on the back of Bertie's head.

SNIP!

"There. All done," he said.

Bertie rolled his eyes. "You haven't started yet!"

"I have!" said Eugene. "You said cut your hair. I cut this one!"

"That's no use," said Bertie. "It has to look shorter all over, or no one'll see the difference."

"How much shorter?"

"I don't know! So it's not in my eyes and sticking up everywhere. Go on!"

Eugene sighed heavily. He grasped a clump of Bertie's hair and raised the scissors.

SNIP! SNIP! SNIP!

CHAPTER 3

Bertie closed his eyes as bits of hair fell to the carpet. He didn't know why he'd never thought of this before. Why bother with hairdressers when you could get a perfectly good haircut in your own home? The two of them could set up in business. Eugene could cut the hair while Bertie took the money.

People would be queuing up. Girls would have to pay double, of course, because they had more hair.

SNIP! SNIP! SNIP!

Eugene paused for a rest. Once you got started, cutting hair was dead easy. You just had to chop away like his dad did when he cut the hedge. He stood back to admire his handiwork.

"Well?" asked Bertie. "How does it look?"

"Er … yeah. Good," said Eugene.

"You have cut it shorter?"

"Oh, yeah. It's definitely shorter."

Bertie stood up and shook off the towel. There seemed to be quite a pile of his hair on the carpet. He went over to take a look in the mirror.

"ARGHHHHHHHHHHH!"

He looked mad! Patches of his hair were missing, while other bits stuck out at all angles.

"What have you done?" he gasped.

"Sorry!" said Eugene. "You asked me to cut it!"

"Not like this! I look like an ALIEN!"

"It's not my fault!" wailed Eugene. "I've never cut hair before. You said you wanted it shorter!"

"I meant shorter all over!" said Bertie. He turned back to the mirror. "What am I going to do?"

Eugene sat down on the bed. "It's not that bad. It'll grow back in a few weeks."

"A FEW WEEKS!" yelled Bertie. This was terrible. He should have known it was no use trusting Eugene. What would his parents say when they saw his hair?

Dirty Bertie

Dad would go mad. Mum would probably faint…

"BERTIE!"

Uh-oh – Dad was calling from downstairs.

"Um … just a minute!" Bertie shouted.

Eugene stared at him in panic. "What shall we do?"

"Bertie! Time to go!" yelled Dad.

Bertie looked around in desperation. They had to hide the evidence quickly. He stuffed the towel and scissors into one of his drawers, and slammed it shut. Help! There were bits of hair all over the carpet. Bertie scooped them up. He looked around for somewhere to hide them.

THUMP! THUMP! THUMP!

Dad was coming up the stairs. Bertie stuffed the hair in the pockets of his jeans.

The door swung open.

"Come on," said Dad. "We need to— ARGH! WHAT HAVE YOU DONE TO YOUR HAIR?"

"This?" said Bertie. "Eugene did it."

"It wasn't my fault! He made me!" cried Eugene.

Bertie shrugged. "You said I needed a haircut, so I've had one."

"I meant at the barber's, not doing it yourself," said Dad. "You look like a moulting sheep!"

He checked his watch. "Come on, we'll just make it. We'll drop Eugene home on the way."

"Where are we going?" asked Bertie.

"To the barber's, where else?"

"But ... but I've already had a haircut!"

"Yes," said Dad. "And now you've got to have another, before your mum gets home!"

CHAPTER 4

Sweeney Bob's didn't have free lollipops
or comics to read. It had three black
leather chairs and one barber – Bob.
Bob had been cutting hair in the same
way for twenty years.

"Who's next?" he growled.

Bertie looked round. The only people
waiting were him, Dad and a pale,

freckle-faced boy.

Bertie looked at him. "After you," he said.

"No, you go," said the boy.

"No, you go. You were here first."

The boy hung his head and plodded over to where Bob was waiting.

"So, what'll it be?" asked Bob, as his victim sat down.

"Um … just a trim, please," squeaked the boy.

Bob reached for his Number One electric clippers. "Short back and sides," he said.

BUZZ, BUZZ, BUZZ!

The clippers hummed. Hunks of red hair fell on the floor. Bertie thought Bob looked more like a boxer than a barber. He had a bulldog neck and razor-short grey hair. His muscly arms were covered in tattoos.

BUZZ, BUZZ, BUZZ!

Bertie shifted nervously in his seat. He glanced at the door, praying for another customer to arrive. He didn't want to face the electric clippers. He'd much rather settle for patchy, sticking-up hair than be bald as a baby's bottom.

Dirty Bertie

The clippers stopped buzzing. The freckle-faced boy got down from the chair, rubbing his neck. He looked like a shaved coconut. Bertie kept his eyes on the floor as the boy paid his money and hurried out. Now there was no escape. Dad was reading the newspaper. Bob swept up the hair on the floor. He set down the broom and cracked his knuckles. *This is it*, thought Bertie. *Goodbye hair.*

"Who's next?" grunted Bob.

Bertie lost his nerve and pointed at Dad. "He is!"

Dad looked up from his newspaper. "What?"

"Take a seat," said Bob.

"No, no, I'm … just waiting," stammered Dad.

"Then it's your turn," said Bob. "Take a seat."

Dad looked round for some means of escape. "Bertie," he pleaded. "You go."

Bertie shook his head. "That's okay. Mum said you needed a haircut."

"Yes, but not…"

"Get a move on," glared Bob. "I'm closing in five minutes."

Dad threw Bertie a dark look. He drooped over to the chair and sat down heavily. Bob draped a grey cloth round his neck.

"Right then, what'll it be?"

"Er … just a very, very light trim, please," said Dad.

Dirty Bertie

Dirty Bertie

Bob switched on his Number One clippers.

"Short back and sides," he said.

BUZZ, BUZZ, BUZZ…

Mum was laying the table for supper when the front door slammed.

"Is that you, Bertie?" she called. "How did you get on?"

Dirty Bertie

"Fine!" said Bertie, bounding into the kitchen.

Mum stared in horror. "Good heavens! What happened to your hair?"

"Eugene cut it," said Bertie, cheerfully.

"What?" cried Mum. "I thought Dad was taking you to the barber's?"

"He did, but Bob didn't have time to cut my hair."

"What? Then whose hair did he cut?"

Bertie grinned and turned towards the door. Dad walked in with a face glowing pink.

"ARGHHHHHH!" screamed Mum.

"It's all right," said Bertie. "It'll probably grow back in a few weeks!"

CHAPTER 1

Bertie loved Saturday mornings.
Saturdays were for watching TV, seeing
his friends or taking Whiffer to the park.
But not today, worst luck. Today he had
to go shopping with Mum. Bertie hated
shopping trips. The shops Mum dragged
him round didn't sell anything he wanted.

This morning they were in Dibble's

Department Store to buy new school shoes.

"Right," said Mum. "Don't touch anything and DON'T go wandering off."

"I won't!" sighed Bertie. Where would he wander off to anyway – to look at bath-mats?

Mum studied the store guide. The shoe department was on the second floor.

"Can we take the lift? Please!" begged Bertie.

"Yes, all right," said Mum, stopping to look at a perfume that was on special offer. Bertie ran ahead and pressed the button marked "Call". He loved going in lifts. He didn't know why his parents hadn't thought of putting in a lift at home. It would save a lot of tramping up- and downstairs when you needed

a chocolate biscuit. He pressed the
button again and held it down.

PING! At last the lift arrived. The
doors slid open and several people got
out. Bertie got in, pleased to have the lift
all to himself. Hang on a minute though,
where was Mum? The doors were
starting to close! He spotted her at the
perfume counter.

"Mum!" shouted Bertie.

"Bertie – wait!" she yelled, dashing over.

Too late – the doors shut in her face. Bertie blinked. He jabbed at one of the buttons on the wall. But instead of the doors opening, the lift gave a sigh and started to go up. *Help! I really am in trouble*, thought Bertie. *Mum will go potty.* He pressed all the buttons at once, but the lift paid no attention.

Finally it stopped with a jolt. PING! The doors slid open and Bertie stepped out. He didn't recognize this floor at all. But before he could change his mind, the lift set off again. Now what? Bertie looked around. Mum would expect him to return to where he'd got lost. That meant the ground floor. Maybe he'd be quicker taking the stairs? He wandered past rows of beds, looking for a sign to point him in the right direction.

Five minutes later, he was still
wandering. Turning a corner, he saw a
large room crowded with people. Rows
of seats were set out facing a long stage,
decked with flowers. *Maybe someone
famous is coming?* thought Bertie. He was
about to ask for help when a shop
assistant appeared. She was wearing a
Dibble's badge with her name: LAURA.

"Thank goodness, there you are!"
she said.

Bertie felt a wave of relief. Mum must
have sent someone to find him. Laura
glanced at her clipboard. "It's Bernie, isn't
it?" she said.

"Er … Bertie," said Bertie.

"Oh sorry, Bertie." Laura checked her
list. It was probably a printing error.
"Anyway, you're here. Hurry up, they're
all waiting."

Bertie looked puzzled.

"Er … sorry, I'm looking for my mum,"
he said.

"Don't worry," said Laura. "She
phoned. She's on her way."

"Is she?"

"Yes, she said she'll meet you here."

Phew! thought Bertie. At least he
wasn't in trouble. Laura opened a door
and ushered him through. "Claudia's

been going up the wall!" she said. "We thought you weren't coming."

Bertie stared. This definitely wasn't the shoe department. It looked more like some kind of changing room. A man was pulling on a shirt. Another hurried by in his pants.

CHAPTER 2

"He's here!" yelled Laura, above the din.
"Claudia, I found him!"

"Thank heaven, darling!" said the lady
called Claudia. She looked down her nose
at Bertie. "You're sure this is the one?"

"Yes, this is Bertie. I found him outside."

Claudia sighed. "Very well, try and do
something with his hair, darling. I'll be

there in a moment."

Bertie frowned. "But I'm only here for new—"

Before he could finish, he was pushed into a chair. A flock of women swooped down on him and set to work. One combed his hair, while another dabbed something on his face and a third tutted over his dirty nails. They all talked at once.

"Head up!"

"Keep still!"

"Look at me, not over there!"

"I need to find my mum," said Bertie, squirming to escape.

"Do you, sweetie?" smiled one of the women.

"Yes, she's meant to meet me here."

"I expect she's out front, waiting to see you."

"Mmm," said Bertie. "Will this take long? Only I'm meant to be getting shoes."

"Don't worry, Claudia will see to it. Look up for me!"

Bertie looked up.

"There!" said the lady. "All done."

Bertie swivelled his chair to look at himself in the mirror. He gasped. He was wearing make-up! His hair stuck up like a paintbrush and he had pink stuff all over his face. He tried to wipe it off with the back of his hand.

Claudia came over to inspect him.

"Well," she sighed. "I suppose he'll
have to do. Where are his clothes?"

"I'm wearing them," said Bertie.

"Not those – they're ghastly!" She
checked her list. "He should be in
sportswear."

Bertie looked at his clothes. They
seemed okay to him. True, his jumper
had got a few splodges of jam on it,
but that was normal. And he was
wearing his best jeans – the ones that

were practically clean.

Claudia was sorting through tops and jackets hanging on a rail. She seized a bright yellow tracksuit with the word DAZZLE written on it.

"Put this on," she commanded.

"Who – me?" asked Bertie.

"Of course you!"

"But I only wanted shoes!"

Claudia snapped her fingers. "Someone bring him some trainers! Why is it all left to me? And please do hurry, darlings, we're on in five minutes!"

The assistants swooped down again. They hurried Bertie into the tracksuit and zipped it up to hide his clothes. It was way too big and a horrible sickly yellow. Bertie thought he looked like a custard cream.

"Super!" said one of the assistants.
"Now let's get these trainers on."

Bertie stared. "I'm not wearing those!"
he cried. "They're for babies."

The assistant glanced at the clock.
"Okay, okay, we don't have time for a
tantrum. Keep your own."

"Excuse me," said Bertie, loudly. "Has
anyone seen my mum?"

But no one took any notice. The music

next door had fallen silent, and an air of anticipation swept through the room. Claudia leaped on to a chair and clapped her hands. "We're starting!" she cried. "Places, darlings, places!"

People started rushing around madly as if a fire alarm had gone off. Bertie found himself herded into a corridor to join a line of people. They were all wearing bright Dazzle sportswear like him. Up ahead was a set of steps leading to a curtained stage.

Claudia clasped her hands in nervous excitement. "Remember, darlings, you are swans, not ducklings! Swans! Good luck!" She blew them all kisses.

The music started up again. Through the curtain Bertie glimpsed rows of people. *Where, oh where, was Mum?*

CHAPTER 3

Mum was on the ground floor and
starting to worry. This wasn't the first
time Bertie had got lost, but in the past
he'd always turned up, looking muddy
and messy or clutching a caterpillar.
This time, however, there was no sign
of him. Dibble's was a huge shop and
Bertie could have been anywhere.

Mum explained this to the kind assistant at the Help Desk.

"And what does he look like?" asked the assistant.

Mum thought. "Small," she said. "With scruffy hair and dirty jeans. Probably a runny nose."

"Runny … nose…" repeated the lady, writing it all down. Mum wished she would write a bit faster.

"And you say his name is…?"

"Bertie," said Mum. "It's my fault – I should never have taken my eyes off him."

The assistant smiled. "I'm sure he can't have gone far. I'll put out a message over the tannoy."

She pushed a button and spoke into a microphone. Her voice carried through the shop.

Dirty Bertie

"Will the little boy called Bertie please come to the Help Desk on the ground floor. His mum is waiting – with a hanky."

Dirty Bertie

Up on the fourth floor, the music was so loud that Bertie didn't hear a word of the announcement. Every now and then someone at the front of the line went up the steps and disappeared from sight. Bursts of applause came from the other side of the curtain. Bertie wondered if the famous person had arrived. Maybe it was a footballer who would sign his shirt?

The others in the line were helping themselves from a box of footballs, tennis rackets and other stuff. Bertie chose a skateboard with go faster stripes. He was nearing the front of the line.

Suddenly, a door opened and a floppy-haired boy burst in.

Dirty Bertie

"Hi!" he panted. "I'm Bernie."

"That's funny," said Bertie. "I'm Bertie."

"Right. Are you in the show? Where's Laura? I'm not too late, am I?"

"Don't ask me," said Bertie. "Everyone here is mad! Late for what?"

"The fashion show, stupid. I'm a model, same as you."

"A model? Ha ha!" hooted Bertie. You'd never catch him prancing up and down a stage in stupid clothes! Hang on a minute … he *was* wearing stupid clothes … and make-up!

Suddenly, the
horrible truth
dawned on him.
This was a
fashion show and
HE WAS IN IT!
ARGHHH!

"Bertie! You're next!" hissed Claudia,
grabbing him by the arm.

"But I…"

Too late, he was pushed through the
curtain.

CHAPTER 4

Bertie gawped at the audience, blinded by the bright spotlights. Millions of people were staring at him. This was a nightmare! There'd obviously been some terrible mistake. That other boy, Bernie, should have been standing up here, not him! Bertie looked around for some way to escape, but Claudia was glaring at him

from the curtain. She waved him
forward on the catwalk where the other
models were striking poses. Bertie
gulped. No way was he doing that. Not
in a custard-yellow tracksuit! It was time
for a speedy exit. He set down the
skateboard, scooted a few steps, and
pushed off hard.

ZOOOOOOM!

He whizzed down the stage, past rows
of surprised faces. The audience clapped,
thinking it was all part of the show.
Bertie looked up and gasped. The other
models had turned round and were
coming back. He was heading straight for
them!

"Out of the way!" he yelled. "I can't…"
CRASH!

He ploughed right into them. The
models scattered into the audience.
A football bounced off a lady in the

front row, squashing her hat.

Bertie sat up and rubbed his head. Luckily, he seemed to be okay. But some of the models were clambering back on to the stage and they didn't look too pleased. Bertie glanced round and saw Claudia advancing towards him. He was trapped … but maybe not. Jumping off the stage, he fled through the audience.

Dirty Bertie

Five minutes later, he reached the ground floor and stood panting for breath. Luckily, no one seemed to have followed him. He unzipped the custard-yellow tracksuit and stuffed it into a nearby bin.

"THERE YOU ARE, BERTIE!" cried a voice.

It was Mum. Never in his life had Bertie felt so glad to see her. She hugged him in relief.

"Where on earth have you been?"

"Oh, um … nowhere special," said Bertie. "I was looking for you."

He decided it was probably better not

to mention the business upstairs with Claudia. Mum would only start asking awkward questions.

"Didn't you hear the announcement?" she said. "They read out your name!"

Bertie shook his head. He hadn't heard anything.

"And what's that on your face – *make-up*?" said Mum.

Bertie turned bright pink. He'd forgotten all about the make-up.

"Er, yes," he said. "I got bored waiting, so I was just … um … trying it on."

Mum frowned. She'd never known Bertie to be interested in make-up before. Still, the main thing was, she'd found him safe and sound.

"Right, just stay out of lifts in future," she said. "Now, let's see about those shoes."

They took the stairs. On the first floor
landing, Mum stopped to read a poster.

"What fun!" she said. "They're holding
a fashion show! Why don't we take a...?
Bertie?"

She looked round. But Bertie had
vanished again.